AWAKENING
VOLUME THREE

Published by
Top Cow Productions, Inc.

CYBER FORCE: AWAKENING, VOL. 3. First printing. September 2019. Published by Image Com
Suite 780, Portland, OR 97210. Copyright © 2019 Top Cow Productions, Inc. All rights rese

AWAKENING
VOLUME THREE

Created by
MARC SILVESTRI

Written by
BRYAN HILL

Art by
ATILIO ROJO

Lettered by
TROY PETERI

Edited by
ELENA SALCEDO

Production by
VINCE VALENTINE & CAREY HALL

Cover Art for this volume by
ATILIO ROJO

CHAPTER NINE

...AND WITH THE GLOBAL BLACKOUT ENDING AROUND THE WORLD, THINGS ARE SLOWLY RETURNING BACK TO NORMAL....
22 CHANNEL
"AN INTERCONNECTED WORLD OF DISCONNECTED PEOPLE.
"ALL OF THEM SEPARATED BY SCREENS.
"NONE PRESENT IN THE MOMENT. ALWAYS THEIR EYES LOOKING OUT DIGITAL WINDOWS.
"COMMUTING LIKE BLOOD CELLS IN A VEIN.
"TOGETHER AND LONELY ALL AT ONCE.
"AN OUTSIDE OBSERVER WOULD THINK WE WORSHIP OUR GLOWING SCREENS LIKE GODS."

AND PERHAPS WE DO.
PERHAPS WE ARE PHARAOH TO THE MASSES. THE GODHEAD THAT SETS CULTURE IN MOTION.
I HAVE A NEW VISION FOR CYBERDATA. A NEW VISION FOR ITS PLACE IN THE WORLD.
THE BLACKOUT TAUGHT THE WORLD HOW MUCH THEY NEED US. NOW LET'S TEACH THEM WHAT OUR PROTECTION REQUIRES.
EVERY GOD HAS LAWS. WHY SHOULD WE BE ANY DIFFERENT?

RIPCLAW!
DAMMIT.
STAND DOWN!
STAND...

IT'S OVER.
CALM DOWN.
YOU ALL RIGHT?
YOU MEAN, AM I VIOLENTLY INSANE?

NO. I'M NOT VIOLENTLY INSANE.
THERE WAS A BOY HERE. THE ONE THEY CALL "WARCHILD."
I NEED TO KNOW WHERE THE BOY IS, RIPCLAW.
YOU BELIEVE I KILLED HIM?
I JUST NEED TO KNOW WHERE HE IS.
I'M NOT JUDGING. I'M ASKING.
GO FIND OUT.
I'LL WAIT.

WELL, THAT'S PLEASANT.
JESUS.
KID.
I CAN HEAR YOUR VITAL SIGNS. YOU DON'T HAVE TO PLAY DEAD. NO ONE IS GOING TO HURT YOU.
WHAT A
YOU?
WE'RE LIKE THE MAN YOU BELIEVED YOU COULD CONTROL.
EXCEPT WE'RE NOT TRYING TO KILL YOU.
WHA
HAPPEN
ME NO

YOU SHOULD HAVE LET ME DIE.
I CAN'T BE THIS.
NO ONE SHOULD BE THIS.
MY HANDS. LOOK AT MY HANDS.
I WAS A SURGEON WITH THESE HANDS.
NOW WHAT AM I? YOU TOOK MY HUMANITY.
AND REPLACED IT WITH WHAT?

YOU WON'T ALWAYS LOOK LIKE THIS. WE'LL TAKE YOU TO CDI AND THEY CAN--
--COVER THIS UP WITH A SHINY OUTFIT AND COLORED HAIR?
WITHOUT OUR INTERVENTION, YOU WOULD HAVE DIED.
AS I UNDERSTAND, GRATITUDE WOULD BE A COMMON RESPONSE FOR VELOCITY'S EFFORTS.
WHAT I WAS DID DIE!
GET OUT.
PLEASE.
CARIN! APH!

DAD!
HE LOOKS LIKE A CHILD. PROBABLY *IS* ONE.
DON'T TREAT HIM LIKE HE'S FRAGILE. HE'S NOT.
HOW'S THE DOCTOR?
SHE'S ALIVE.
AND SHE HATES ME FOR IT.
SHE'LL GET OVER IT.
WHAT ARE WE SUPPOSED TO DO WITH A PRETEEN EVIL GENIUS?
TAKE HIM TO THE REST OF THE EVIL GENIUSES.

CLICK
STRYKER. INCOMING. CODE. ZETA. FIVE. JUPITER.
MORGAN STRYKER. PLEASED TO SPEAK WITH YOU.
NEW VOICE. I'M NOT USED TO NEW VOICES.
CALL ME LILITH.
JOB'S DONE. BOY IS IN OUR CUSTODY. A DOCTOR NEEDS YOUR HELP. APH STABILIZED HER, BUT IT'S ALL CRUDE.
EXCELLENT WORK.
BRING THEM ALL TO CDI. YOU AND I NEED TO HAVE A CONVERSATION ABOUT THE FUTURE.

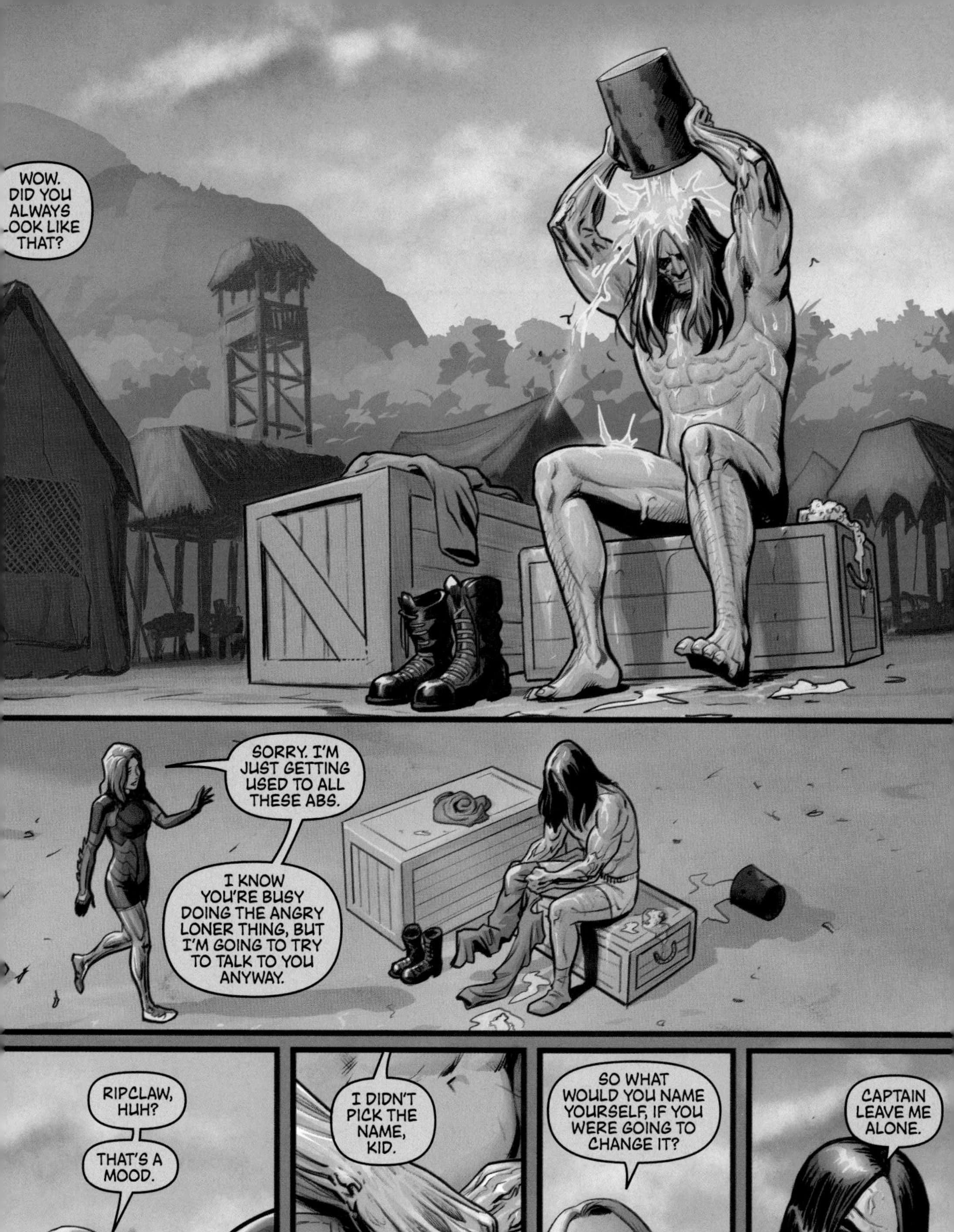
WOW. DID YOU ALWAYS LOOK LIKE THAT?
SORRY. I'M JUST GETTING USED TO ALL THESE ABS.
I KNOW YOU'RE BUSY DOING THE ANGRY LONER THING, BUT I'M GOING TO TRY TO TALK TO YOU ANYWAY.

RIPCLAW, HUH?
THAT'S A MOOD.

I DIDN'T PICK THE NAME, KID.

SO WHAT WOULD YOU NAME YOURSELF, IF YOU WERE GOING TO CHANGE IT?

CAPTAIN LEAVE ME ALONE.

YOU SHOULD LAUGH, KID. THAT WAS FUNNY.
I'M JUST SURPRISED YOU TOLD A JOKE.
DON'T GET TO KNOW ME. I'M NOT COMING BACK WITH YOU.
TELL YOUR FATHER HE'S BEING USED. THAT "GOOD SOLDIER" THING WON'T MATTER.
THAT "GOOD SOLDIER" THING IS ALL I TRUST.
YOU SHOULD TRY TRUSTING SOMEONE.
WHAT MAKES YOU THINK I HAVEN'T?

YOU DON'T EVEN KNOW IF THAT'S GOING TO WORK.

IT COULD JUST PUNCH A HOLE IN YOUR HEAD. AND YOU'D BE ALIVE TO FEEL ALL OF IT.
WHY DON'T YOU JUST GO AHEAD AND GIVE THAT TO ME, DOMINIQUE.
I WOULD PREFER YOU NOT HAVE A SMOKING HOLE IN YOUR HEAD.
YOU'RE THE ONLY PERSON HERE THAT I LIKE.
IT GETS BETTER. THE POWER HELPS. FEELING WHAT YOU CAN DO.
I PROMISE YOU IT GETS BETTER.
EVERYTHING HURTS, BUT I CAN'T *FEEL* IT. I JUST *KNOW* IT.
IT'S LIKE I'M HIDING INSIDE OF A SHELL.
THEY CHANGED YOUR BODY. NOT YOUR SOUL.

WHAT YOU ARE ISN'T THE FLESH.
THE BODY IS NOTHING.
THE SPIRIT IS WHAT MATTERS.
I'M SCARED.
I'M
CARED
M GOING
O WANT
THIS.
HOW ABOUT A DEAL? IF YOU GO WITH THEM, I'LL GO WITH THEM.
AND NEITHER ONE OF US HAS TO BE SCARED ALONE.

Orders incoming.
Confirm receipt of new protocols.
NEW PROTOCOLS CONFIRMED.
AND UNDERSTO

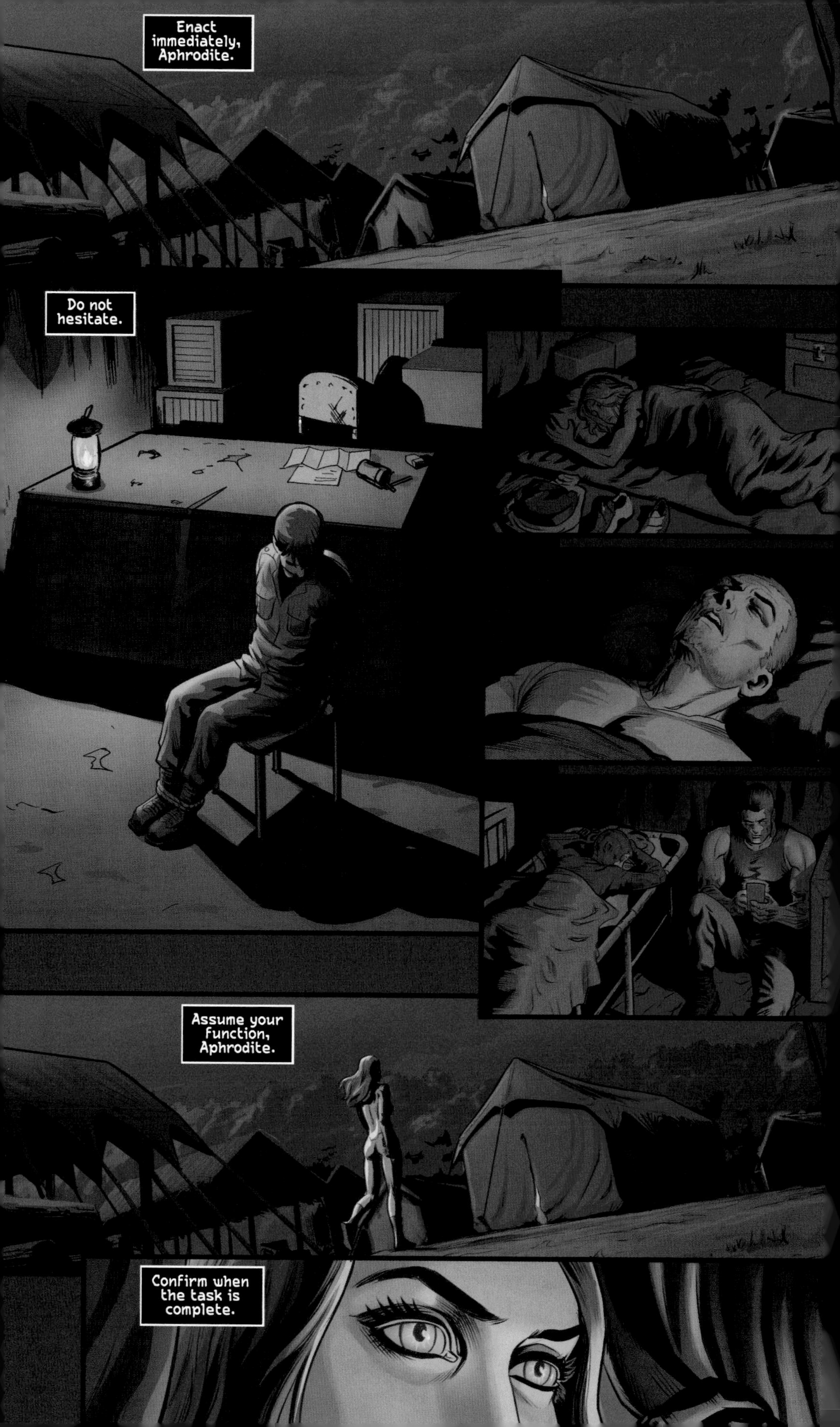
Enact immediately, Aphrodite.
Do not hesitate.
Assume your function, Aphrodite.
Confirm when the task is complete.

UNDERSTOOD.
WAIT. PLEASE!
PLEASE! DON'T!
I'LL BE GOOD!
I PROMISE, I'LL BE GOOD!

THIS WON'T HURT.
CLOSE YOUR EYES.
SCHRAAKKK
THANK YOU, RIPCLAW.
I DIDN'T WANT TO DO THAT. I JUST DIDN'T HAVE A CHOICE.
I KNOW.

SHE WAS GOING TO KILL ME! ***KILL HER!***
SETTLE DOWN, BOY.
I HEARD RIPCLAW APPROACHING. I ASSUMED HIS INTENTION WAS TO STOP ME. I STALLED UNTIL HE COULD.
IS THAT TRUE?
ACCURATE ENOUGH.
WE'RE GOING BACK TO CDI. TELL STRYKER THAT.
I'M GOING WITH HIM.
AND I'M GOING TO BURN IT ALL DOWN.
AND WE' ALL GOIN BE FRE

CHAPTER TEN

OI HEADQUARTERS.
"THE WORLD IS ON AGAIN. RIPCLAW HAS RETURNED TO OUR CARE.
"WELL DONE, MORGAN STRYKER."
AND WHAT HAPPENS TO HIM NOW?
HE WILL BE DEBRIEFED AND REMINDED OF HIS DEBT.
01001011
VOICE ONLY
WHAT DEBT?
HE OWES US LIFE. ALL OF YOU DO.
ALL WE ASK FOR IN RETURN IS LOYALTY.
LOYALTY GOES BOTH WAYS. IT'S SOMETHING YOU EARN.
RIPCLAW THINKS YOU'RE THE ENEMY OF THE WORLD. WHY SHOULDN'T HE?

"THERE ARE TWO GODS, STRYKER.
"THE ONE THAT CREATED THE WORLD, THAT CREATED MANKIND AND GAVE HIM FREE WILL.
"TWO GODS. ONE BOOK.
"THE FIRST IS FEARED, FOR HE BRINGS THE GREAT FLOOD AND THE PLAGUES.
"THE SECOND IS LOVED, FOR HE IS SEEN AS LOVE.
"BUT IN TRUTH, THERE IS ONLY *ONE* GOD.
"ONE GOD THAT CAN BE LOVED AND FEARED ALL AT ONCE.
"CONSIDER US AS *GOD.*
"FEAR US, IF YOU MUST.
"BUT LOVE US JUST AS MUCH."

WHAT ARE YOU DOING TO HIM?!
01001011
VOICE ONLY
RE-EDUCATING HIM ON HIS PURPOSE.
I HOPE THIS IS A LESSON THAT YOU HAVE ALREADY BEEN LEARNING, MORGAN.
BUT THERE IS TIME TO TEACH YOU TOO.
01001011
VOICE ONLY
I WANT TO SEE HIM.
YOU WILL.
ONCE HE HAS FOUND HIS WAY BACK TO GRACE.
01001011

ALMOST HUMAN.

YOU LOOK GREAT, DOM.
AND YOU CAN DO GREAT THINGS. JUST LIKE ME AND DAD.
I ALMOST CAN'T REMEMBER WHAT IT'S LIKE TO NEED A CHAIR.
MY HANDS ARE NUMB.
IT'LL PASS. YOUR NERVOUS SYSTEM IS RECALIBRATING TO YOUR NEW LIMBS.
I DIDN'T FEEL MY FEET FOR A WEEK.
THEY'RE NOT YOUR FEET ANYMORE.
THESE AREN'T OUR BODIES.

THEY ARE, DOM. YOU'RE STILL YOU.
I'M STILL ME.
AND RIPCLAW IS WHAT? WHERE?
WE'RE WEAPONS. THINGS. CAN'T YOU UNDERSTAND THAT?
I UNDERSTAND THAT WE HAVE THE POWER TO HELP THE WORLD.
WE ONL HAVE TH POWER THAT TH GIVE US
I'M NOT GOING TO BE DEPRESSED THAT YOU'RE STILL ALIVE, DOM. LIFE IS GOOD. NO MATTER WHO GIVES IT TO YOU.
WE'RE ALIVE. LET'S *FEEL* ALIVE. LET'S *BE* ALIVE.
WHEREVER RIPCLAW IS, I'M SURE HE'S FINE. THEY SPENT NEARLY A BILLION DOLLARS MAKING HIM WHAT HE IS.
THEY WOULDN'T PUT HIM IN A DUNGEON.

WARNING. SUBJECT IS ACTIVE.
WARNING. CONTAINMENT INTEGRITY AT 25 PERCENT.
WARNING.
WARNING.
SUBJECT IS MOVING.
WARNING.

RASSSH
WARNING. SUBJECT IS ACTIVE.
STRYKER.
NTAINMENT
BREACH.
CKDOWN IN
EFFECT.
RIPCLAW.
I NEED TO FIND YOU BEFORE THEY DO.
SKRISSS
THOOOOM
RIPCLAW. STAND DOWN.
STAN
DOWN

RIPCLAW. RETURN TO CONTAINMENT.
SECURITY PROTOCOLS ARE BEING NOTIFIED.
RETURN TO CONTAINMENT--
--TO PREVENT INCIDENT.
BUT I *WANT* AN *INCIDENT.*
AND I WANT TO SEE THE FACE OF GOD.
RIPCLAW!

STOP.
MOVE, LITTLE GIRL.
I HATE THEM AS MUCH AS YOU DO, BUT WE CAN'T WIN A WAR.
NOT HERE.
COME WITH US.
MOVE OR I WILL MOVE YOU!
I CAME BACK FOR *ONE THING.*

AND I'M GOING TO TEAR THIS PLACE APART.
WE CAN'T BEAT THEM, RIPCLAW.
I KNOW YOU KNOW THAT.
YOU'RE THE ONLY ONE HERE I TRUST.
SO TRUST *ME.*
AAAHHH!
RAKKKK
IT HAS TO END, DOMINIQUE. ALL OF IT. US. *THIS.*
LET ME END IT.

SUBJECT DEEMED ACTIVE THREAT.
YOU MAY USE LETHAL FORCE.
STAND DOWN OR WE WILL FIRE.
NO! STOP!
WE'RE TALKING TO HIM!

STEP AWAY FROM THE SUBJECT.
I DON'T KNOW WHAT CAN DO, BUT E'LL ALL FIND OUT IF YOU ORCE ME TO SHOW YOU.
PUT THE GUNS AWAY!
LET THEM KEEP THEM.
I WANT THEM TO KNOW THEIR GUNS CAN'T SAVE THEM.
RAAAAAAAAAHHHHHHH!

ARRRRRGH!
ZZZSSAK
RIPCLAW, I'M SORRY!
I... DON'T EVEN KNOW...WHAT I JUST DID.
SUBJECT UNCONSCIOUS.
THREAT NEUTRALIZED.
WELL DONE, SUBJECT.
NOW GO BACK TO YOUR CHAMBERS.

NO!
KRASSSSSHHH
UGNH!
AAAHH!
DOM! WHAT ARE YOU DOING?!
I DON'T...

RIPCLAW!
LOOKS LIKE I'M LATE. YOU OKAY, CARIN?
WHAT HAPPENED?
UM...SHE HIT HIM WITH THE PURPLE THING. THEN SHE HIT THE GUARDS WITH THE PURPLE THING.
DAD, I HONESTLY DON'T KNOW WHAT'S HAPPENING.
HE'S STABLE. VITALS ARE STABLE.
RIPCLAW. I'M SORRY. I KNOW YOU'RE RIGHT.
WE CAN'T BE WHAT THEY WANT US TO BE.

BUT I DON'T KNOW WHAT WE ARE.
TAKE MY HAND. YOU'RE MY PATIENT NOW.

THEY DON'T TOUCH YOU WITHOUT ME THERE.
YOU HAVE MY WORD.
Off line
THE WORD OF A DOCTOR--
AGAINST THE WORD OF GOD.
HISTORY NEVER CHANGES.
BUT THE VISION IS CLEAR.

I'M LATE TO THE RAGE PARTY, BUT I'M ASSUMING YOU WANT TO KILL EVERYTHING?
THEY'LL KEEP DOING THIS TO PEOPLE UNLESS WE STOP THEM!
WE CAN MAKE THIS A GOOD THING.
STAND DOWN! ALL OF YOU!
CALM DOWN, TIN MEN. WE'RE HAVING A CONVERSATION.
I GO WHERE HE GOES. I OBSERVE WHATEVER YOU'RE GOING TO DO TO HIM.
RIPCLAW?
SHE'S MY DOCTOR. SHE CAN SPEAK FOR ME.
I TRUST HER.
LET THEM TRUST EACH OTHER. LOVE IS JUST ANOTHER SYSTEM OF CONTROL.
GENTLEMEN--

"--I BELIEVE WE'VE FOUND HIS WEAKNESS.
"ALLOW THEM TO RETURN TO THEIR QUARTERS.
"GOD HAS PLANS FOR THEM."

CHAPTER ELEVEN

THIS IS THE MOST DIFFICULT PART.
THE SHARING OF THE VISION.
THE CONSENSUS.
THERE'S ALWAYS A LITTLE RESISTANCE TO THE TRUTH.
JUST A LITTLE.
BUT EVENTUALLY--

"IT WILL ALL MAKE SENSE, RIPCLAW.
"YOU JUST NEED TO SEE WHAT I SEE."

"FAMILY.
"THE FARM AND THE HUNT.
"THE MOMENT OF THE KILL.
"THE WEIGHT OF CONSCIENCE.
"THE HAUNT OF MEMORY."

I CAN RELIEVE YOU OF IT ALL.
NO MORE PAIN.
THERE IS FREEDOM IN EMBRACING YOUR FUNCTION, RIPCLAW.
DREAM OF THAT.

I'M A DOCTOR. AND I'M NOT. A WOMAN. AND I'M NOT.
YOU'LL GET USED TO IT.
WHAT ARE THEY DOING TO RIPCLAW?
YOU DON'T WANT TO THINK ABOUT THAT.
I WANT TO STOP IT, MORGAN.
SO DO I.
THEN WHY AREN'T YOU?

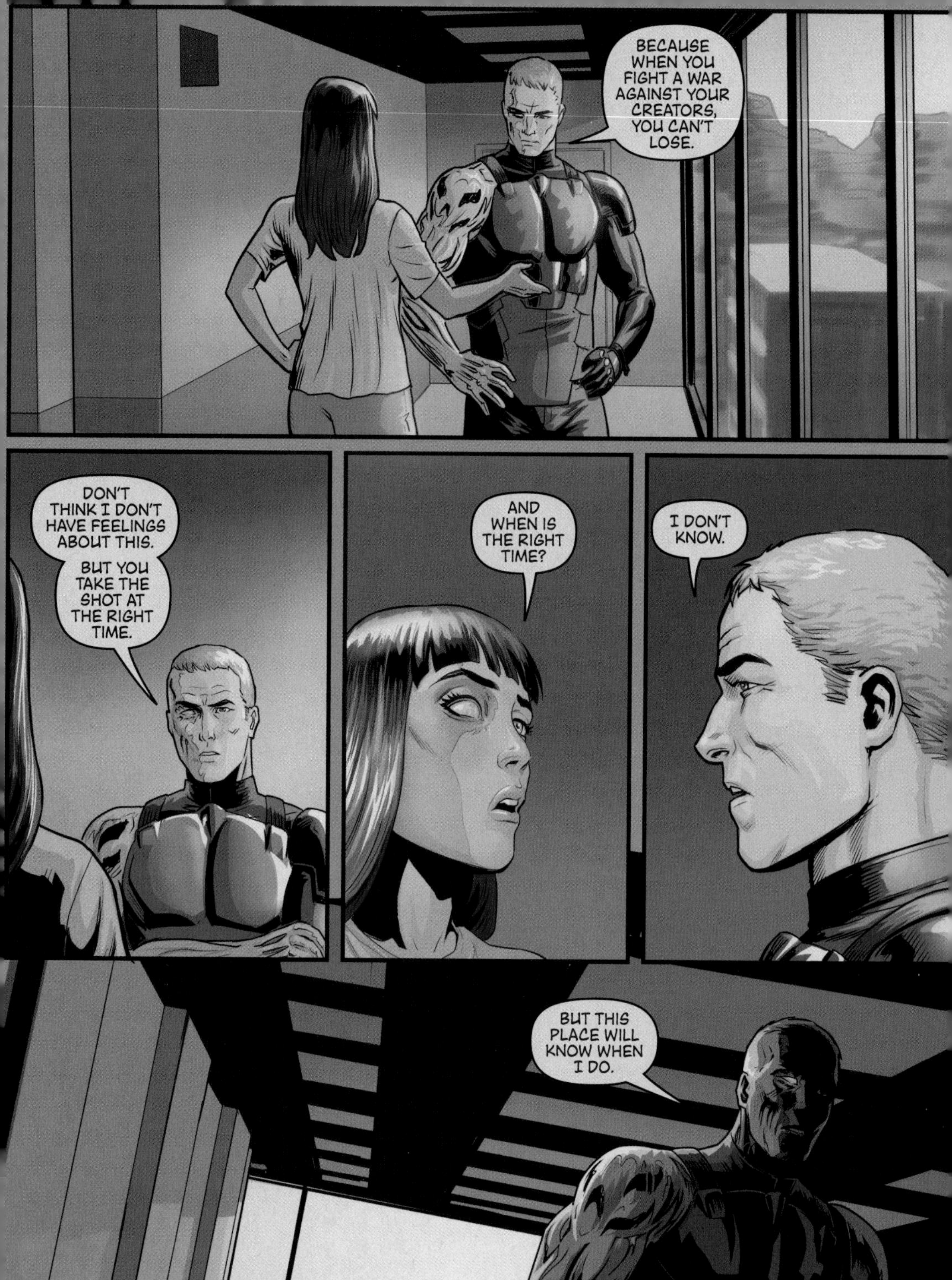
BECAUSE WHEN YOU FIGHT A WAR AGAINST YOUR CREATORS, YOU CAN'T LOSE.
DON'T THINK I DON'T HAVE FEELINGS ABOUT THIS.
BUT YOU TAKE THE SHOT AT THE RIGHT TIME.
AND WHEN IS THE RIGHT TIME?
I DON'T KNOW.

BUT THIS PLACE WILL KNOW WHEN I DO.

ISOLATE THE INFLUENCE PROTOCOLS.
BUILD THE FIREWALL.
SHIFT: AGGRESSIVE.
CLINK
FIND RIPCLAW.

KRASSSSSHH

GREETINGS.
THOK
KRAKKK
UGHN!
MORGAN. COMMENCE.
I'M IN MOTION.

COPY, APHRODITE.
CARIN AND I ARE INCOMING.
DID APH CALL IT?

LAST CHANCE, CARIN. WE DON'T HAVE TO DO THIS.
WHAT *ELSE* CAN WE DO, DAD?

WHEN YOU MOVE. MOVE *FAST.*
DAD.
WHAT ELSE CA I DO?

CRACK
MORGAN. I HAVE EYES ON HIM.
INITIATE CEREBRAL BOOST.
WAKE UP, RIPCLAW.
...APH...
DID SHE BREAK YOU?
NOT EVEN CLOSE.

STAND DOWN!
I'D RATHER NOT.
YOU UP FOR THIS?
ENOUGH.
STAND DOWN OR I WILL FIRE!
YOU MAY WANT TO STAND BACK, GREEN.

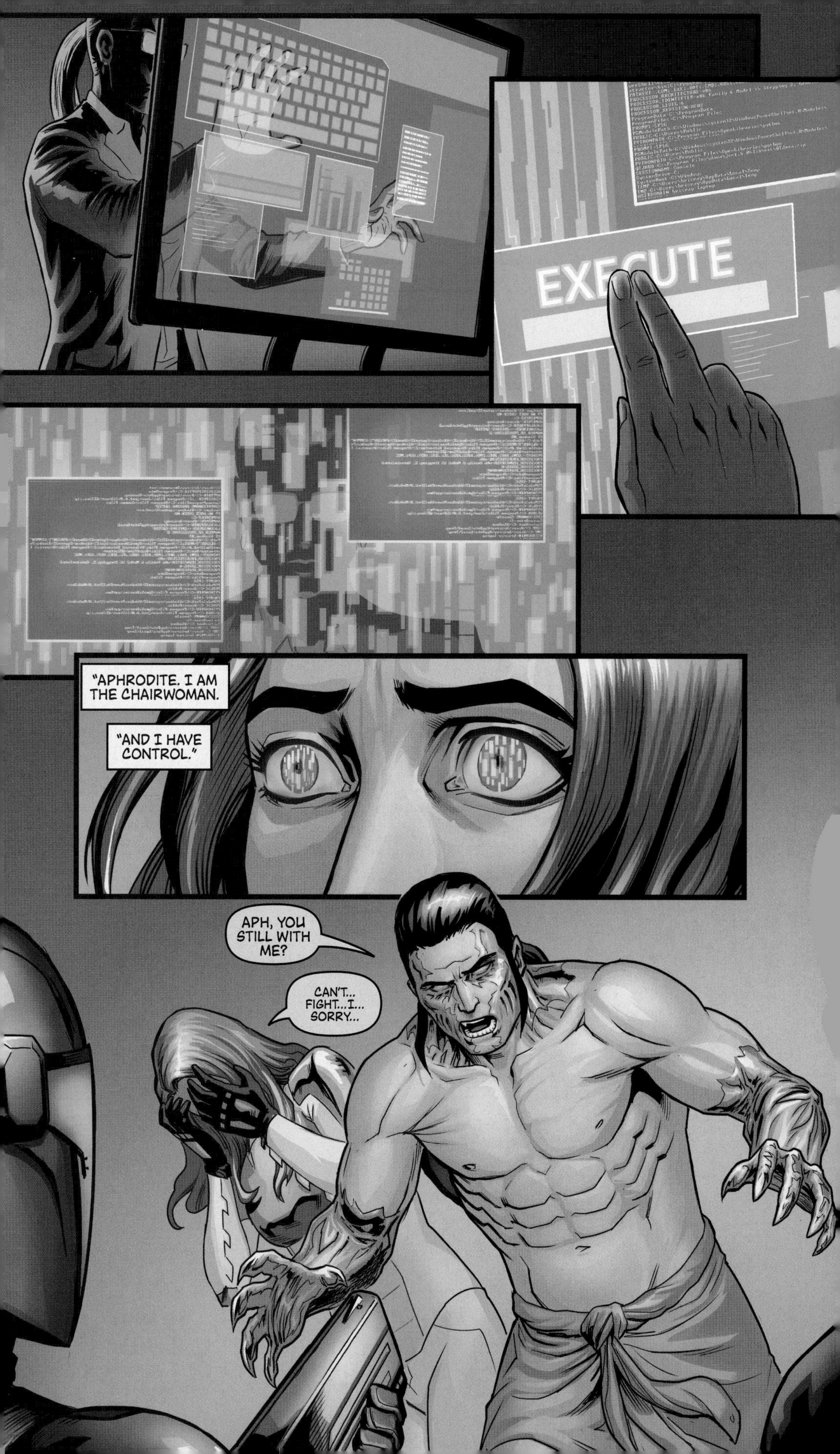
EXECUTE
"APHRODITE. I AM THE CHAIRWOMAN.
"AND I HAVE CONTROL."
APH, YOU STILL WITH ME?
CAN'T... FIGHT...I... SORRY...

WHACK
KRUNCH
WHACK
WHACK

I...
...WANT...
SLITCH
...MY MIND BACK!
PLITCH
APH. YOU OKAY?
THAT LOOKED GROSS.

I'M NOT...
...ONE HUNDRED PERCENT.
WHAT PERCENT DO YOU NEED TO BE TO KILL OUR WAY OUT OF HERE?
THAT, I CAN DO.

CARIN.
GET READY TO RUN.

HOWDY.
THIS IS THE PART WHEN I TELL YOU TO DROP THE WEAPONS.
AND THEN YOU WON'T.
THEN YOU SAY--
DON'T MOVE!
THEN I DO WHAT I SHOULD HAVE DONE THIRTY SECONDS AGO.
RAKAKAKAKAKAKAKAK

MADAM CHAIRWOMAN. ADVISE.
LET THEM GO.
I LEFT RIPCLAW ALONE FOR A REASON.
"I ANTICIPATED THIS.
KRAK
"THEIR DESIRE FOR FREEDOM.
"THEY'RE DOING NOTHING WE CAN'T REBUILD.
"THEY'RE GOING NOWHERE THEY CAN'T BE FOUND."

GET TO THE BOMBER. MOVE FAST.
WHIRRRRRRMMMMMM
"THEY'RE THE FUTURE. NO MATTER HOW CONFUSED THEY ARE ABOUT IT."
FSSSSHHHHHHHHHH
AND THE WORLD WILL TEACH THEM--

THAT THE FUTURE BELONGS TO US.
DAD. WHERE ARE WE GOING?
SOMEWHERE FAR.
"TRACK THEM. STUDY THEM. AND WHEN IT'S TIME--
"WE'LL WAKE THEM FROM THEIR DREAM OF FREEDOM.
"AND BEND THEIR KNEES TO WHAT IS YET TO COME."

MATT HAWKINS

TWITTER: @topcowmatt
FACEBOOK: http://www.facebook.com/selfloathingnarcissist

A veteran of the initial Image Comics launch, Matt started his career in cor book publishing in 1993 and has been working with Image as a creator, writer a executive for over 20 years. President/COO of Top Cow since 1998, Matt has crea and written over 30 new franchises for Top Cow and Image including *Think Tank*, *Tithe*, *Necromancer*, *VICE*, *Lady Pendragon*, *Aphrodite IX*, and *Tales of Honor*, as v as handling the company's business affairs.

BRYAN HILL

TWITTER: @bryanedwardhill
INSTAGRAM: bryanehill

Writes comics, writes movies, and makes films. He lives and works in Los Angel

ATILIO ROJO

FACEBOOK: http://www.facebook.com/atilio.rojo.52

Atilio Rojo has been writing and drawing erotic comics since 2002. Rojo is b known for his work on *Transformers*, *G.I. Joe*, *Snake Eyes*, *Dungeons and Drag* *LOD*, *IXth Generation*, *Eden's Fall*, and *Samaritan: Veritas* (*The Tithe*).

RITTEN BY
CON GLASER

RT BY
ARA KNAEPEN

ETTERS BY
ROY PETERI

OW #IMAGECOMICS #TOPCOW

GECOMICS.COM ▪ TOPCOW.COM

I learned a new word recently··insomnia.
It's an old relic I found in a half-corrupted database·· it means the inability to sleep.

Today, the word is meaningless. we don't need to sleep··not physically, anyway.

However, I'm glad I found it, because through furtive research, it led me to another word I find very fitting for my current situation:

ntmare.

My name is Rust·· one of the few cyborgs living in the ruins of Speros City who lasted long enough to get a nickname besides "hey, you."
GET DOWN HERE, YOU MORON!
WUH--!
WHERE THE HELL WERE YOU?! WE NEEDED EVERYONE FOR THIS!
I WAS... REGROUPING.
REGROUPING?! WE HAD THEM! WHATEVER, TAKE THIS AND FOLLOW ME!

Most cyborgs are like Daz--they've never known anything but this fight, the constant struggle to secure even the basic needs of life and civilization.
This is all they know to do--they've never been shown anything different.
Not me, though-- I remember something else.
ARE YOU COMING? WE DON'T HAVE MUCH TIME.

I remember her.
TAKE MY HAND AND WE'LL GET OUT OF HERE.

WE'RE READY TO GO!
CONFIRM COORDINATES--NEW CYTHERA.
Confirmed - Launching.
I HEARD WE'RE GOING TO A PARADISE.
"PARADISE"? WHAT'S THAT?
IT'S SUPPOSED TO BE A PLACE WHERE YOU CAN DO ANYTHING YOU WANT--NO FEAR OF ARES.
THAT'S RIGHT--PEOPLE NEED TO SEE THAT THEY DON'T HAVE TO PICK SIDES IN A POINTLESS WAR JUST TO STAY ALIVE. MY CITY IS A PLACE WHERE YOU CAN DREAM A LITTLE. CITIZENS OF MY CITY CAN CHOOSE WHAT THEY WANT TO DO--THEIR DESIRES, PROFESSIONS.
WHAT'S THAT MEAN?
IT MEANS YOU'RE FREE NOW.
NO--I MEAN, WHAT'S "DREAM" MEAN?

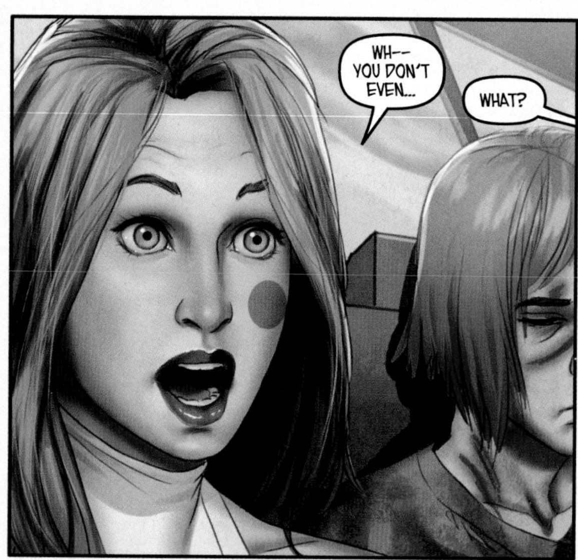
WH-- YOU DON'T EVEN...
WHAT?

SHOULD... SHOULD I KNOW THAT?
LOOK-- DO YOU HAVE ANY... THOUGHTS? MEMORIES OF THINGS THAT MAKE YOU HAPPY?
YEAH.

WHEN DO YOU THINK ABOUT THEM?
I-I DON'T KNOW, WHENEVER I...I DON'T KNOW.
WHAT ABOUT WHEN YOU'RE ASLEEP?
WHEN I'M A WHAT?

LOOK--LEAN BACK, CLOSE YOUR EYES, AND TRY TO THINK ABOUT NOTHING FOR A WHILE. THAT SHOULD HELP EXPLAIN THINGS.

"Think about nothing"? What did that even mean?
How do you even do that?
Think about nothing...
Maybe later.

OH, NO... NO...
HOW DID HE FIND US? I THOUGHT THIS WAS A STEALTH SHIP!
UNKNOWN, MA'AM, BUT AT THE MOMENT, THAT'S NOT REALLY IMPORTANT...

YOU TRIED TO TAKE SOMETHING OF MINE. YOU WILL RETURN IT. THIS IS *NOT* A REQUEST.

BRING THAT SHUTTLE DOWN. EITHER THEY COME BACK ALIVE, OR YOU SCRAPE THEM OFF THE GROUND. NO ONE STEALS FROM ARES!
WHY CAN'T YOU LET THEM GO? AREN'T THERE ENOUGH PEOPLE IN YOUR CITY TO TREAT LIKE ANIMALS?
NEVER ENOUGH-- AND I KNOW IT HURTS YOU.
WE'RE TAKING THESE PEOPLE WITH US. I'VE NEVER FEARED YOU BEFORE AND I WON'T START NOW.
YOU SHOULD.

NO!

YOU DARED TO ATTEMPT ESCAPE FROM MY TERRITORY. THEY PAID WITH THEIR LIVES AND GOT OFF EASY. I ALMOST REGRET THAT THE WORST PUNISHMENT I CAN THINK OF DOESN'T NEED ME TO DO ANYTHING.
ONCE YOU TASTE FREEDOM, NOTHING STINGS MORE THAN HAVING IT RIPPED AWAY. YOU ARE MINE AND SO IT WILL BE FOREVER.
YOU MET HER, AND HOPED. NOW YO WILL FACE ME, AND DESPAIR BEYOND BEING SAVED.

Even through all that, I remember tasting sleep for the first time-- enough to learn more.
RUST! WHERE'D YOU GO NOW?

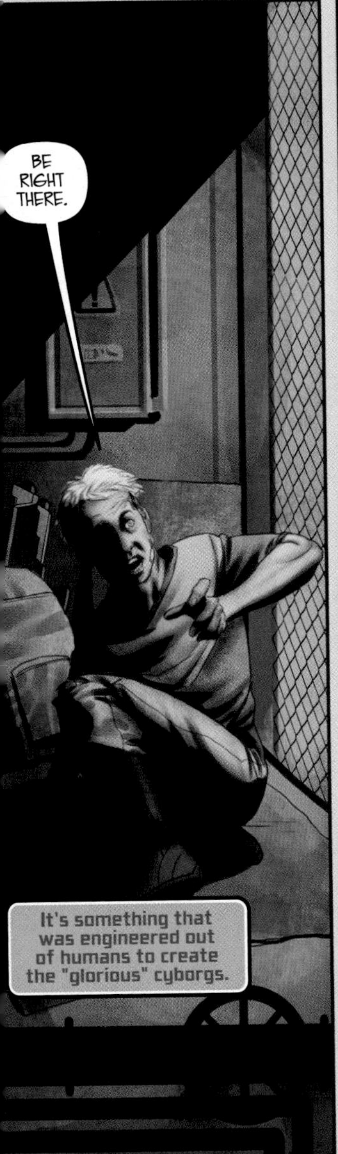
BE RIGHT THERE.
It's something that was engineered out of humans to create the "glorious" cyborgs.

An improvement from when our culture of celebrating life fully converted to despising death.

Sleep was, by their reasoning, a step closer to death than waking, and had to go. Except they never accounted for the need to dream.
Speros
City Map

Their solution was "networking"-- syncing up with a system that stabilizes your brain...somehow.
...except it never worked all that great.
peros
City Map

Ares' rule didn't exactly help-- it's causing more instability...like Daz.

I was one of them. Until recently, I never knew anything else, and allowed my mind to erode.

Until the day I met her, and she showed me how to dream.

Since that day, I've learned what sleep is. My mind has been allowed to dream.
I can see a place where I don't have to split my time between fighting, running to a fight and nothing else.
It's right at the end of this tunnel.
URGH--!

...which is the same as saying it's on the other side of the goddamn moon.
LET ME GO, DAZ.
YOU WERE JUST GOING TO LEAVE? WHEN WE WERE SO CLOSE TO WINNING?
WINNING WHAT? OUR FIGHT WAS ALWAYS POINTLESS. THERE'S SOMETHING BETTER.
BETTER THAN TAKING BACK OUR HOME? OUR PRIDE AS CYBORGS?!
We have no pride. We were made to serve -- our entire existence a cruel joke.
Out there was something real. A chance to reclaim the life that everyone here has forgotten, or never even knew.

Don't blame him.
HE'S ALL YOURS.
After all, meeting her was pure dumb luck--I could have stayed trapped just as easily as him. Might have been better, even.
I wouldn't have this burning ache to get out and meet my savior--show her I learned to dream.
But I know it's going to happen again--I just need another chance. I need to be smarter this time.

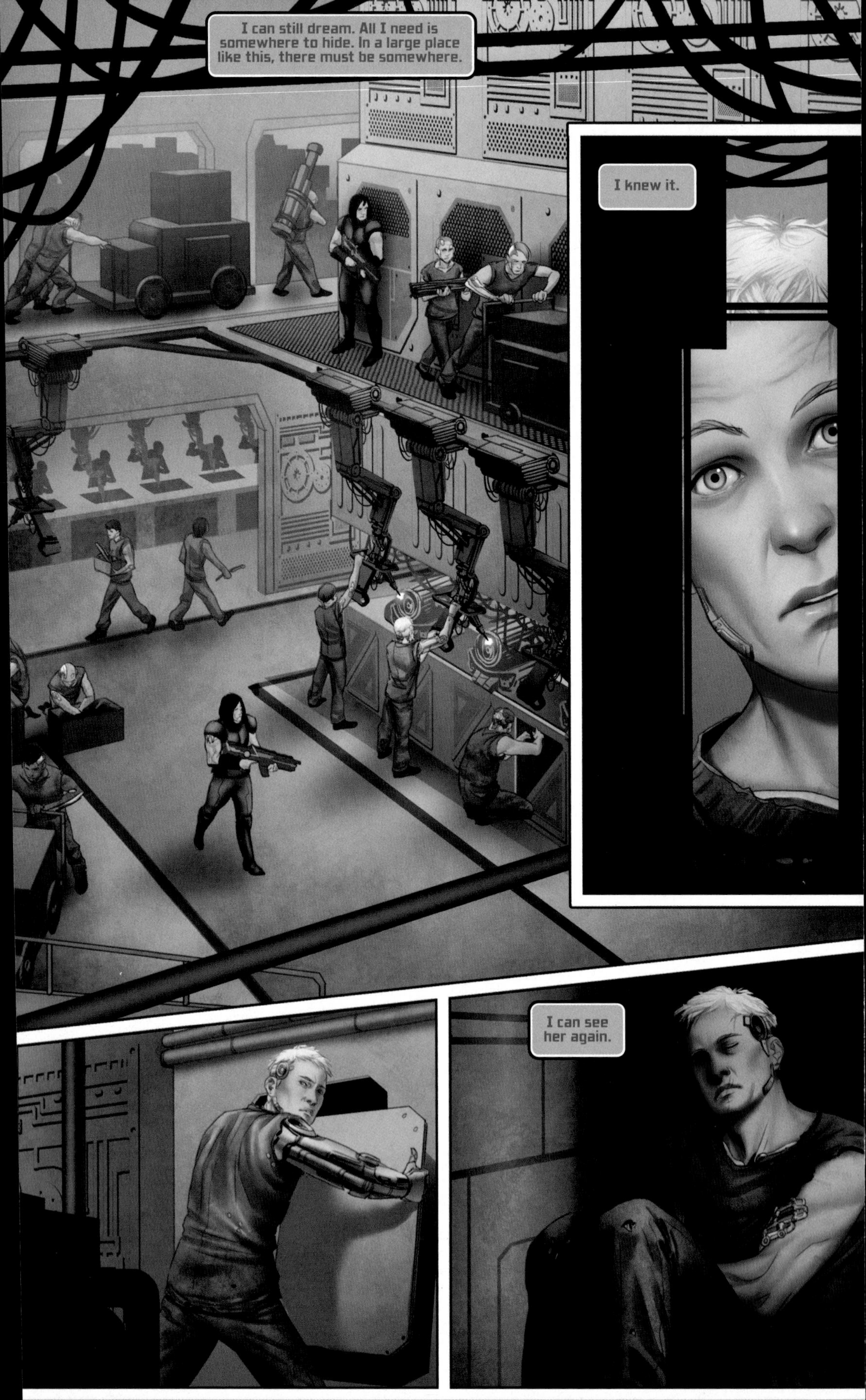
I can still dream. All I need is somewhere to hide. In a large place like this, there must be somewhere.
I knew it.
I can see her again.

HOW DOES IT LOOK?
IT WOULD TAKE AN INVASION TO BREAK THEM OUT-- NO TELLING HOW MANY WOULD DIE IF WE TRIED TO SAVE THEM.
SO WE DO NOTHING?
FOR NOW. WE'LL NEED A REAL PLAN TO GET IN THERE AND RESCUE ARES' "PETS." A FRONTAL ATTACK WOULD HAVE THE EXACT OPPOSITE RESULT.
"HOPEFULLY SOMEONE CAN DREAM UP A WAY OUT FOR THEM."
END.

“IMMORTAL LONGINGS”

WRITTEN BY
JOANNA MARSH

ART BY
MARCO RENNA

COLORS BY
CHRIS NORTHROP

LETTERS BY
TROY PETERI

EW CYTHERA
OF COURSE THAT'S A POSSIBILITY, BUT...NO, MAYBE... WOULDN'T THAT MAKE HER NEURONS EXPLODE?
ARGH!
HMPH. I KNOW THAT WAS COUNTERPRODUCTIVE. I SUGGEST YOU IGNORE IT AND GET TO WORK, AS I INTEND TO.
I THINK I'D ONLY EMBARRASS MYSELF.
OH MY...YOU! THAT IS, MY LADY! I AM SO SORRY ABOUT THAT DISPLAY OF IRRATIONAL WEAKNESS AND--
NO, DON'T APOLOGIZE. AND... DON'T BOW. IT'S DAFNE, ISN'T IT?

SUCH A MESS IN HERE--
YOU KNOW MY NAME.

I TRY TO KNOW MY PEOPLE. YOU FLED HERE FROM NEW APOLLONIA, I THINK?

I DID! I WAS BRILLIANT THERE! I MEAN...I'M TRYING TO USE MY TALENTS TO SHOW MY GRATITUDE.
I'VE HEARD.
IX

I'VE BEEN WORKING FROM THE GROUND UP, TRYING TO RECREATE THE RESURRECTION CHAMBERS. IT'S BEEN TRYING, BUT I CAN DO IT!
IX
I DON'T DOUBT IT.
BUT I THINK YOUR TALENTS WOULD BE BETTER SERVED ELSEWHERE.

ARE YOU DOUBTING MY INTELLECT?
THAT IS, WHAT PURPOSE COULD BE BETTER THAN GIVING YOU BACK YOUR IMMORTALITY?
HELPING THE PEOPLE HERE. IMPROVING THEIR LIVES.
BY...NOT PROTECTING YOURS?
YOU REMEMBER LIFE IN NEW APOLLONIA.
...YES.
LIVING IN FEAR OF ATTACK BY MY BROTHERS AND SISTERS AS THEY PLAYED GOD.
LIFE AND DEATH WAS A GAME TO THEM BECAUSE THEY DIDN'T HAVE THAT FEAR.

I'M NOT A GOD. I'M JUST LIKE YOU.

...I DOUBT THAT, MY LADY.
BUT I'M SURE I CAN REPURPOSE MY EXISTING RESEARCH.

THANK YOU.
I'M SO GLAD YOU'RE HERE TO HELP.
HOW DID IT GO, MA'AM?
VERY WELL.

MAY I ASK YOU SOMETHING?
ANYTHIN
MA'AM

DO YOU
BELIEVE
THE SOUL

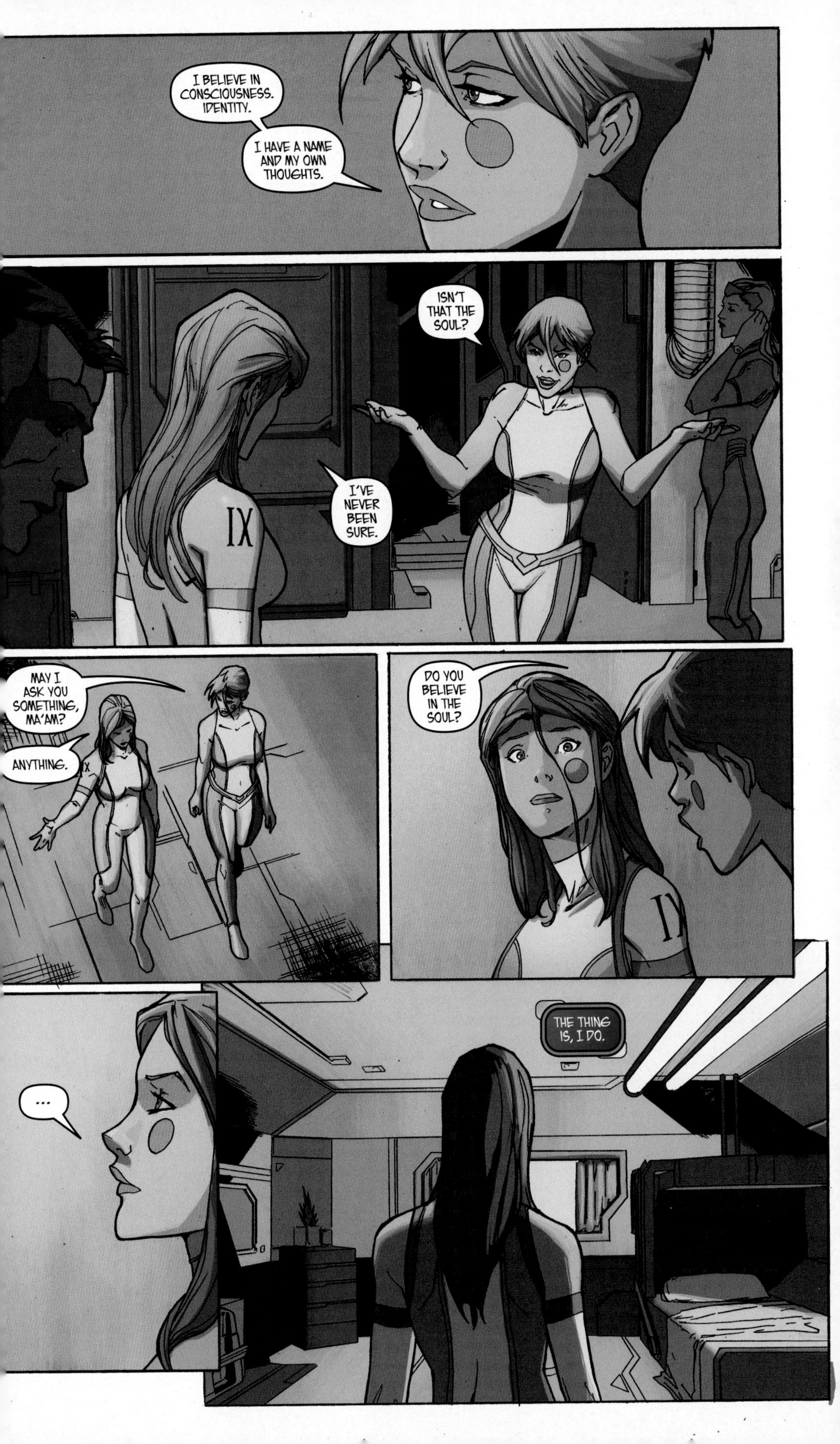
I BELIEVE IN CONSCIOUSNESS. IDENTITY.
I HAVE A NAME AND MY OWN THOUGHTS.
ISN'T THAT THE SOUL?
I'VE NEVER BEEN SURE.
MAY I ASK YOU SOMETHING, MA'AM?
ANYTHING.
DO YOU BELIEVE IN THE SOUL?
THE THING IS, I DO.
...

I BELIEVE THE SOUL EXISTS AND GOES TO A NEW PLACE WHEN YOU DIE.
I'VE ALWAYS DOUBTED THE RESURRECTION CHAMBERS TRULY RETAINED THE SOUL FROM BODY TO BODY.
CLICK
STILL...
THERE'S A CHANCE IT MIGHT KEEP ME FROM A PLACE WHERE ALL MY FAMILY IS HAPPY AND TOGETHER.
I'M TOO SELFISH TO RISK THAT.
HOW MORTAL OF ME.
END

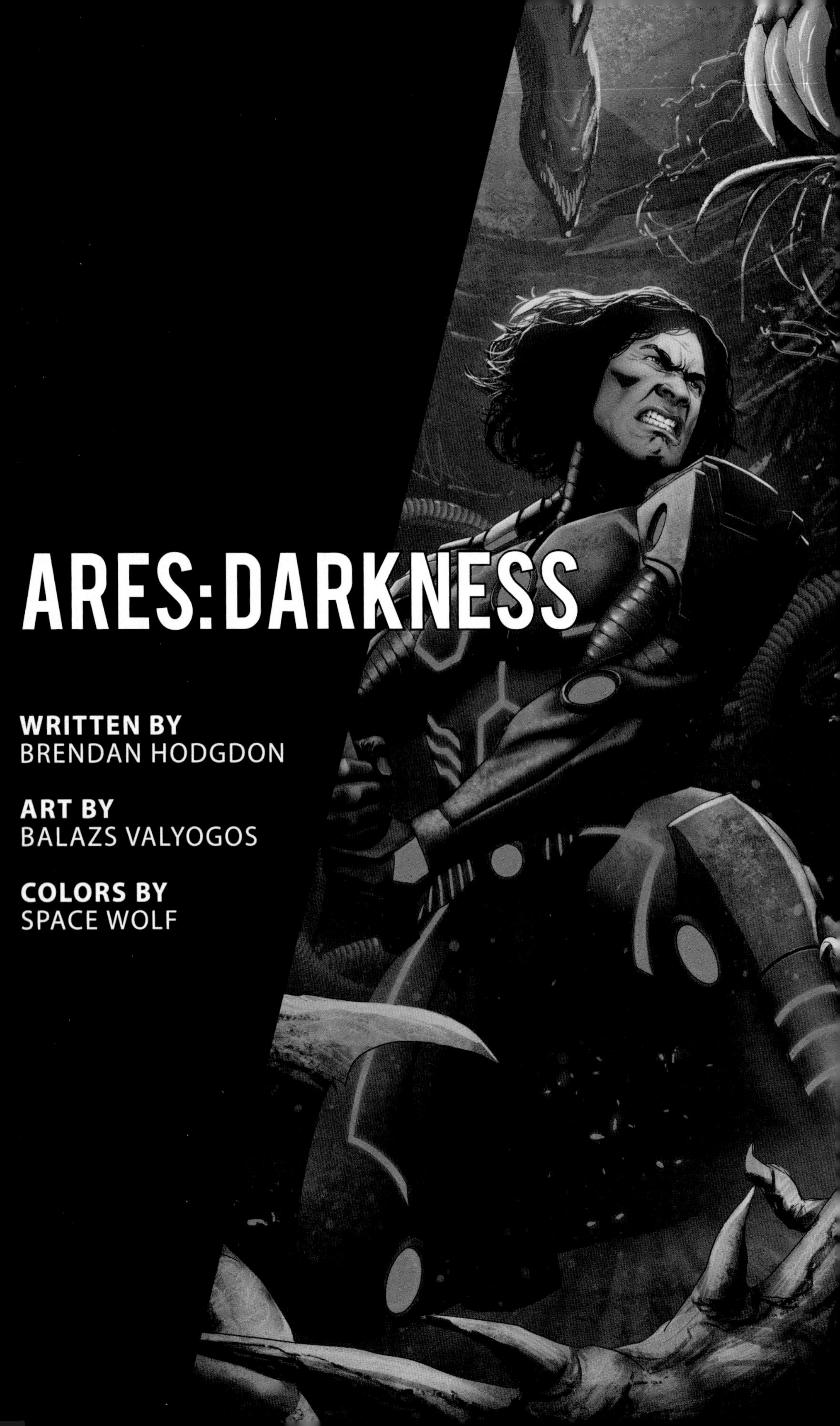

ARES: DARKNESS

WRITTEN BY
BRENDAN HODGDON

ART BY
BALAZS VALYOGOS

COLORS BY
SPACE WOLF

IT BEGAN THE DAY OF THE ASCENSION.
BRRRRT BRRRRRT
ER WE FACED ...*CREATURE* HEPHAESTUS' SANCTUARY.
BRRRRT
BRRRRT
WHAT THE HELL ***WAS*** THAT?
JUST SOME DUMB MUTANT ANIMAL. NOTHING TO WORRY ABOUT.
I FELT A *COLDNESS* CREEPING ALONG MY SPINE. ONE I HADN'T FELT IN YEARS.
THIS TIME, THE COLD STAYED...
...AND I *REMEMBERED.*

I HAD FELT THIS COLD BEFORE.
IN MY CHILDHOOD.
YOU DID WELL, ARES.
VERY WELL, INDEED.
BUT IMAGINE WHAT ELSE YOU COULD DO...
IF YOU CLAIMED THIS POWER FOR YOURSELF.

GAHHHH!
SIR...?
ARE YOU ALRIGHT?
YES... I'M FINE...
THESE VISIONS HAVE BECKONED ME EVERY DAY FOR MONTHS.
OW IT'S TIME TO FIND OUT WHY.
SIERRA MUNOZ.
VVVVRROOOMMMMM
I AM TO MAINTAIN MY SUPREMACY AMONG THE IXS...
...I NEED TO RID MYSELF OF THIS CURSE.
I CANNOT ALLOW MYSELF TO BE MADE WEAK BY THESE DISTRACTIONS.
MY ONLY OPTION S TO FOLLOW THE VISIONS IN MY HEAD...
...TO GO TO THE PLACE MY DREAMS SHOW ME, NIGHT AFTER NIGHT.

CHASING GHOSTS TO THE ENDS OF THE EARTH.
SIR, ARE YOU SURE YOU DON'T WANT US--?
NO.
BUT WE DON'T KNOW WHAT'S IN THERE...
WHY NOT BRING BACKUP?
BECAUSE IT WOULDN'T BE SPORTING.
DO YOU THINK ATHENA WOULD FACE A MYSTERY LIKE THIS WITH HELP? OR POSEIDON? DO YOU DOUBT I'M STRONGER THAN THEM?
NO, OF COURSE NOT--
THEN I GO ALONE.
WAIT FOR ME.
XV

KRAKK
THE FIRST THING YOU NOTICE IS THE STENCH OF SULFUR IN THE AIR.
WHAT IN THE HELL -- ?
IT IS FAR FROM THE LAST THING YOU NOTICE.
WHY AM I HERE?
BECAUSE, ARES...
YOU HAVE TO SEE.

I KNOW THAT VOICE.
FROM MY DREAMS.
NOW IT CALLS ME INTO THE SHADOWS HERE.
RIGHT WHERE IT WANTS ME TO BE.
I CAN ALREADY HEAR ATHENA'S DERISIVE LAUGHTER.
THE MOCKERY I WOULD ENDURE IF SHE SAW ME NOW, ON THIS WILD GOOSE CHASE.
BUT I WILL NOT BE DETERRED.
I DON'T KNOW WHAT THIS HAUNTING IN MY MIND IS.
I DON'T KNOW WHY IT'S LED ME TO THIS PLACE.
WHATEVER THE REASON...

...I'M READY FOR ANSWERS.
YOU AREN'T READY FOR A THING.
HAHAHAHA...
OH ARES--
YOU.
WHY HAVE YOU BROUGHT ME HERE?
TO SHOW YOU THE TRUTH.
I THINK YOU'RE MISTAKEN.
ALL I SEE HERE...
...IS DEATH!
PCHOW PCHOW PCHOW

PCHOW-PCHOW-PCHOW
THOSE WEAPONS OF YOURS WON'T HELP YOU WITH ME.
I'M NOT REALLY HERE, ARES.
I'M A SLIVER IN YOUR MIND, A FRAGMENT LEFT BEHIND--
--YEARS AGO BY MY TRUE SELF.
WAIT...
...IN THE LAB...
YES.
I'VE BEEN RIGHT HERE WITH YOU EVER SINCE.
I KNOW EVERYTHING ABOUT YOU.
I KNOW YOUR FEARS, YOUR ASPIRATIONS...
AND I KNOW WHAT YOU ARE MEANT TO BE.
BUT FIRST--

--YOU AVE TO E WHAT OU ARE.

I DON'T KNOW WHAT HAT LITTLE BITCH DID TO ME, BUT--
I'VE *SAVED* YOU, ARES.

GRRRRRR!

YOU JUST DON'T REALIZE IT YET.

THAT'S IT...

GETTING WARMER...

ALMOST THERE...

AH. *FINALLY.*

YOU GET TO SEE THE TRUTH.
AND WHAT TRUTH IS THAT?
THAT YOU'VE BEEN PLAYED FOR A FOOL, ARES.
JUST AS SHE WAS.
IX
JUST AS WHO WAS?
SSSSSSSSSS
SSSSSSSSSSSS

GRRAARRGHH!
I--?
KA-THUCK
CLA-CLICK-CLACK
I HOPE I'M WRONG ABOUT YOU, ARES.
I'D RATHER NOT SEE YOU *FAIL*.
LITTLE GIRL...

...ENOUGH!
NOT YE LITTLE BOY.
I'VE NEVER BEEN HIT BY ANYTHING LIKE THAT BEFORE.
NONE OF MY SIBLINGS COME CLOSE TO THIS SORT OF STRENGTH.
YES, ARES...
NONE OF YOU HAVE POWER LIKE THIS.
HSSSSSSSSSSSS
OR PERHAPS NOT.
BUT YOU COULD CHANGE THAT.

QUIET, SPECTER.

GAHHHH!

SSSSSSSSARGH!
KRUNCH

I WON'T LET THIS BEAST DEFEAT ME.
SWISH
I WON'T LET THAT GREMLIN IN MY MIND UNDERMINE ME.
THOCK
I AM BRED FOR WAR AND COMBAT.
I AM THE BEST OF THE IXs.
THE STRONGEST.
I CANNOT BE DEFEA--
ARGH!

H
ES.
OU THINK
HAT YOUR
AINING WAS
MAKE YOU
TRONG?
SILLY CHILD.
YOUR ENHANCED ABILITIES EXIST ONLY TO MAKE YOU A PAWN.
YOU WERE ANOTHER EXPERIMENT IN YOUR MOTHER'S QUEST TO LIVE FOREVER.
YOU'RE NO BETTER THAN THAT MONSTER OVER THERE.
LOOK AT HER.
ALL OF THAT POWER, RELEGATED TO BEING A SEX OBJECT AND SCIENCE EXPERIMENT TO ANCIENT IDIOTS. LUCKY TO SURVIVE.
SHE COULD HAVE BEEN SO MUCH MORE.
AND SO CAN YOU.

IF YOU EARN IT.
HISSSSSSSSSSKK
KRA-KRACKK
OOOFFF!
GRRRRRR
GET UP, GET UP, GET UP...

TIME'S UP, ARES.
SHIT.
KR-KRACK
KRRRRREEEAAK
KRRRRA-KA-KICKKK
AAAAAAAARRGGHHH--!

YOU SAID I COULD BE MORE.
HOW?
THE POWER THAT BIRTHED HER...
THAT BIRTHED ME...
IT WILL COME TO YOU, IN TIME.
WHEN IT DOES, YOU WILL FACE A CHOICE.
YOU CAN SUBMIT TO THE R THE CHAIRWOM INTENDED FOR YOU...REMAIN PAWN AS ELLE HERE DID...
OR YOU CAN U THAT POWER F YOURSELF.
BECOME THE GOD DESERVE BE.
AND RESTOR THE NATU ORDE OF THE WORLD
THE CHOICE IS YOURS.

WE'RE *DONE* HERE.
LET'S GO.
I WANT TO BELIEVE I'VE GONE INSANE.
THAT THE GIRL IS A FIGMENT OF MY IMAGINATION.
BUT TRUTHFULLY SHE'S NOT.

SHE HAS HER OWN AGENDA.
FOR ALL HER TALK OF *FREEING* ME FROM THE CHAIRWOMAN'S SCHEMES...

...THE *POWER* THAT CREATED HER PROBABLY HAS SCHEMES OF ITS OWN.
PERHAPS IT'S JUST USING ME AS WELL.

THAT'S *FINE*.
WE HAVE MORE THAN ENOUGH IN COMMON.
JUST *IMAGINE*...

...WHAT WE COULD ACCOMPLISH TOGETHER.
END

“A GRAVE MEETING”

WRITTEN BY
CHARLES CRAPO

ART BY
MARK WHITAKER

LETTERS BY
TROY PETERI

2820 AD
WHY ARE YOU DRAGGING ME TO A GRAVEYARD IN THE MIDDLE OF THE NIGHT?
SOME OF US SLEEP, YOU KNOW.
THERE ARE SOME THINGS, HADES, THAT MUST BE DONE IN THE DARK.
THERE IS SOMETHING I LEFT UNFINISHED HERE LONG AGO.
AS YOUR MOTHER ONCE WRONGED ME, I ONCE WRONGED THE MEMORY OF MY OWN.
IN MY YOUTH, I STILL DIDN'T KNOW MY POWERS. I--
WHATEVER.
I'M NOT HERE TO HEAR YOUR LIFE STORY.
JUST TELL ME WHAT TO DO SO I CAN GET SOME SLEEP.
I'VE EXPLAINED WHAT NEEDS TO BE DONE TO THESE TWO DARKLINGS.
I'M SENDING THEM ALONG TO AID YOU.
DON'T WAIT UP, BOSS. THIS DAME AND ME MIGHT HAVE TROUBLE KEEPING OUR HANDS TO OURSELVES.
IF YOU HAVE ANY TROUBLE, I'LL RIP YOUR HANDS OFF.

SO, HADES, DO YOU LIKE SMALL GUYS?
NO. WHERE IS THIS THING WE'RE LOOKING FOR?
YOU LITTLE...
KEEP YOUR DAMN HANDS TO YOURSELF!
THUWOP
!
OUCH.
I GUESS I DESERVED THAT.
HERE LIES JENNY ESTACADO
OH.
I FOUND WHAT WE'RE LOOKING FOR.

OKAY, START DIGGING.
ME?
YOU WANT ME TO GET BLISTERS ON THESE BEAUTIFUL HANDS?
WELL, I'M NOT DIGGING SO WHO IS?
ISN'T THAT WHY WE BROUGHT MUSCLES ALONG?
YOU'RE NOT AS DUMB AS YOU LOOK.
THANKS.
YOU WANNA MAKE OUT WHILE HE DIGS?
DO YOU WANT ME TO HIT YOU AGAIN?
NO THANK YOU.
WHAT THE HELL IS THAT THING?

SPLOOSH!
SHKRIP
IT KILLED MUSCLES?
WHAT THE HELL WERE THOSE MUSCLES FOR IF HE COULDN'T FIGHT?
I'M NOT SURE WHAT YOUR BOSS IS UP TO...
...BUT
THEN I'M PROBABLY KICKING YOURS.
AND IF I'M STILL IN THE MOOD, I'M KICKING YOUR BOSS'S.

I CAN'T BELIEVE IT KILLED MUSCLES.
WE'RE ALL GONNA DIE!
WELL, TIME TO GET OUT OF HERE BEFORE THAT THING KILLS HER AND COMES AFTER ME.
GET IT, HADES!
I BELIEVE IN YOU!
TOO BAD SHE HAD TO DIE BEFORE I COULD BANG HER.

I CAN STILL HEAR YOU, YOU LITTLE IDIOT.

DON'T DIE, HADES.
I LOVE YOU!
DING!

SPLISH
EMPTY...
...WAS THIS SOME SORT OF TEST?
THE BOSS MOVES IN MYSTERIOUS WAYS.
WANNA DO IT IN THE COFFIN BEFORE WE GO BACK?
JUST SHUT UP BEFORE I KILL YOU.
END

COVER GALLERY

ISSUE #9 COVER
ATILIO ROJO

ISSUE #10 COVER
ATILIO ROJO

ISSUE #11 COVER
RAFFAELE IENCO
RAFF
IENCO

APHRODITE IX: ARES COVER
SARA KNAEPEN

ARES: DARKNESS COVER
SARA KNAEPEN

PINUP BY BALAZS VALYOGOS